KNAPSACKS

Joris-Karl Huysmans (1848-1907) published two overlapping collections of prose poems, *Le drageoir aux épices* (1874) and *Croquis Parisiens* (1880; tr. as *Parisian Sketches*), producing two Naturalist novels, *Marthe* (1876) and *Les Soeurs Vatard* (1879) in between. *À rebours* (Charpentier, 1884) represented a dramatic change of direction, and became the handbook of Decadent lifestyle fantasy. *Là-Bas* (1891), based on the author's flirtation with the Parisian Occult Revival, became equally archetypal in its fascinated but horrified account of contemporary Satanism. The author dressed as a monk for the rest of his semi-reclusive life.

J.-K. HUYSMANS

KNAPSACKS

translated by
Henry Roche

THIS IS A SNUGGLY BOOK

ISBN: 978-1-943813-77-3

This edition of Knapsacks is a reprint of the translation originally published in 1928. The text, however, has been corrected, and slightly revised.

KNAPSACKS

A S soon as I had ended my studies, my parents thought it right to make me appear before a table covered with green cloth at which sat several old gentlemen anxious to inquire if I was sufficiently acquainted with dead languages to be promoted to the degree of Bachelor of Arts.

My examination proved satisfactory. A dinner, to which were invited all the elders of the family, celebrated my success. They expressed anxiety as to my future, and decided that I was to study law.

I managed to, pass the first examination fairly well and spent the allowance for my second year's tuition fees with a fair-haired damsel who showed me her affection intermittently.

I frequented with assiduity the Quartier Latin, where I learned many things, among others to take an interest in the students who every evening, over their drinks, gave vent to their political views, and to get acquainted with the works of George Sand, Heine, Edgar Guinet and Henri Mürger.

I had reached the age of doing foolish things. This lasted about a year; the fruit of youth was ripening: the electoral contests at the close of the Empire left me cold; I was not the son of a senator, nor of an exile, and had only to maintain, under any kind of government, the traditions of mediocrity and penury which had long been followed by the family.

I had little taste for law. The Code, thought I, had been purposely drawn up with a view to furnishing certain people with the opportunity of arguing about its most insignificant details. It seems to me even now that no clearly written sentences could reasonably give occasion to such different interpretations.

I was trying hard to choose a not too distasteful profession when the late Emperor found one for me: his bungling policy made me a soldier.

The war with Prussia broke out. To speak the truth, I did not understand what motives made this slaughter of men necessary. I felt no desire to kill others or to be killed by them. I was, however, enlisted among the Mobile Guards of the Seine

and was ordered to report at 7 p.m. at the barracks in the Rue de Lourcine as soon as I had been
provided with uniform and boots.

I was there punctually. After roll-call part of the
regiment rushed out and filled the street. Crowds
surged and wine-shops were filled in no time.

Huddled together, workmen in their smocks,
workwomen in tatters, soldiers in belts and gai-
ters, unarmed, beat time with clashing glasses to
the Marseillaise which they yelled out of tune. In
their incredibly high képis provided with peaks
resembling a blind man's shade, and tricoloured
tin cockades, in dark blue tunics, with scarlet
collars and braid, and light blue trousers with a
red stripe, the Mobiles of the Seine howled at the
moon before starting for the conquest of Prussia.

The uproar in the wine-shops was deafening,
a hurly-burly of glasses, water-bottles, shouts, interrupted at times by the rattling of the windows
beaten by the wind. The rolling of a drum was
suddenly heard above the din. From the barracks
issued forth a fresh column; then followed inde-
scribable revelling and tippling. The soldiers who
were drinking in the shops rushed out accompanied by their relatives and friends, who vied for
the honour of carrying their knapsacks; the ranks
were broken up; it became a jumble of soldiers

and citizens; mothers wept; fathers, less emotional, smelled of wine, while children jumped with joy and with their shrill voices shouted patriotic songs!

They went through Paris in disorder amid flashes of lightning, whose white zigzags lashed the tumultuous clouds.

Suffocating was the heat, heavy were the knapsacks. They stopped to drink at every street corner and at last reached the station at Aubervilliers. An interval of silence was broken by the sound of sobs that were again hushed by the howling of the Marseillaise, and we were at length driven into trucks like cattle. "Good-night, Jules! Goodbye! Mind you be good! Above all write to me!" We shook hands a last time, a whistle sounded: the station was behind us.

About fifty men had been shoved into our rolling truck: some shed bitter tears and were gibed at by others who, downright drunk, fixed lighted candles in their ammunition boxes and yelled at the top of their voices: "Down with Badinguet! Long live Rochefort!" Several were silent and dejected in a corner and kept their eyes on the floor that shook, raising a cloud of dust. The train suddenly halted and I got down. The night was dark—twenty-five minutes past midnight. Fields extended in all directions and afar, lit up by the flashes of lightning, a small house or a tree stood out suddenly on the stormy sky. Nothing was heard but the roar of the engine, out of whose funnel flew clouds of sparks which were scattered along the train like a bouquet of fireworks. We all alighted and went up to the engine, which loomed larger in the darkness and seemed immense. The halt lasted at least two hours. The signals shone out red and the driver was waiting for them to be changed. When they turned white we got into the trucks. Then a man ran up waving a lantern: he said a few words to the guard, who at once shunted the train to a siding, where we again stood still. None of us knew our whereabouts. I got down once more, and was sitting on an embankment nibbling at a bit of bread and having a drink, when a dreadful hurricane came rushing from afar, roaring and spitting flames as it approached. It was an interminable artillery train passing at full speed, loaded with horses, men and cannon whose bronze necks gleamed in the welter of lights. Five minutes after, we moved on slowly, the halts becoming longer and longer. At last day broke, and leaning out of the window, fatigued by my night's shaking, I looked at the country around and beheld a succession of chalky plains stretching as far as the horizon, and a streak of pale green the colour of sickly turquoise, a flat, dull, unfertile region called Barren Champagne.

Gradually the sun waxed warmer; we rolled on and at last got to our destination! Having left the evening before at eight, we reached Châlons the next day at three. Two of the Mobiles were left behind: one had been pitched into a river from the top of a car and the other smashed his head against the edge of a bridge. The comrades having pillaged the sheds and gardens they had visited during the stoppages of the train, yawned, with lips puffed by wine and swollen eyes, or else played at throwing at each other from the end of the truck the stalks of shrubs, or the hencoops they had stolen.

The arrival proved as disorderly as the departure had been. Nothing was ready: no canteen, no straw, no cloaks nor arms; we only found tents full of dung and lice left by troops just sent on to the frontier. We subsisted as well as we could, for three days, eating a saveloy one day, drinking a bowl of coffee and milk another, unmercifully fleeced by the inhabitants, passing the night anyhow without straw or covering. This was not the way to make us appreciate the profession inflicted upon us.

As soon as they were billeted, the travelling companions separated: working men were placed in tents with other working men; men of a better class congregated in like manner. In my tent we were well assorted, as we had managed to get rid of two fellows after making them drunk: they had smelt greatly in need of a foot-bath in consequence of prolonged and voluntary neglect of hygiene.

A day or two passed. We had to mount guard with pointed sticks; we were given plenty of brandy; the erstwhile starvelings were now decently fed; suddenly Marshal Canrobert ordered a grand review. I can see him on his high charger, bent down on the saddle, his hair blown about by the wind, his waxed moustache standing out on his pallid face. A mutiny broke out. Our wants were disregarded, and far from being persuaded by the Marshal that we were well looked after, we shouted in chorus, when he threatened to repress our complaints by force: "Rataplan, rataplan! Shoot a hundred thousand men! To Paris, to Paris!" Canrobert turned livid and cried out, reining in his horse in our midst: "Hats off to a Marshal of France!" Again the ranks hooted. Then, turning his charger, and followed by his scandalized staff, he threatened us with his finger, hissing between his clenched teeth: "You'll pay dearly for this, my little Parisians!"

Two days after this scene the icy camp water made me so ill that I was hurried off to hospital. Buckling up my knapsack after the doctor's examination, in charge of a corporal, I crawled away, dragging my legs and perspiring under my accoutrements. The hospital being cram-full, I was not admitted. So I betook myself to one of the nearest field ambulances, where, one bed being vacant, I was received. At last I unloaded my knapsack, and until the moment when the chief surgeon would forbid me to stir I strolled about the little garden which connected the various buildings. A door suddenly gave passage to a man with a voluminous beard and sea-green eyes. He plunged his hands into the pockets of a long gambier-coloured cassock and cried out from far off as he perceived me: "Eh! my man, what are you doing here?"

I went up to him and explained why I had come. He only gesticulated with his arms and shouted: "Not before they have given you your hospital clothes will you be allowed to walk in the garden." I returned to the house, where an attendant provided me with a long cassock, trousers, slippers and a long cap. I looked at myself in my little pocket mirror and realized what a fright I was. What a face! What a get-up! My eyes were sunken, my complexion pale, my hair clipped short, my nose shiny in its protuberant parts. Add to all this my long mouse-coloured cassock, my trousers of a ruddy yellow, my huge flat slippers, my gigantic cotton cap. In truth I cut an extremely ugly figure; I laughed outright and turned towards my nearest bed-fellow, a tall fellow of Jewish type, who was sketching my portrait in his notebook. We at once became friends. I told him my name was Eugène Lejantel; he replied that his was Francis Emonot. As we both knew a certain artist, we started an aesthetic conversation which made us forget our misfortunes. In the evening, boiled beef with black lentils was distributed; they gave us full glasses of clear liquorice-water. After this meal I undressed, glad to be able to stretch myself in a bed, rid of my uniform and my boots.

The next morning at six o'clock I was roused by a loud slam of the door and by noisy voices. I sat up, rubbed my eyes and perceived the gentleman I had seen last evening in his gambier-coloured overall, advancing majestically, followed by a train of assistants. It was the chief surgeon.

He had hardly entered the room when, rolling his dull green eyes from right to left and from left to right, he thrust his hands into his pockets and shouted:

"Number one, show your leg, your dirty leg! Ah! that leg is not doing well; the wound is running like a stream. Pure water-lotion, lint, half rations, a good liquorice tea."

"Number two, show your throat, your dirty throat! It's getting worse and worse. Tomorrow we must remove those tonsils."

"But, doctor . . . !"

"What! Am I speaking to you? If you add another word, I shall put you on a strict diet."

"But still . . ."

"This man to be kept on a strict diet! Write down: diet, gargling, a good liquorice tea."

Such was his way of examining the patients, prescribing his good liquorice tea for every case, whether venereal disease, fever or dysentery.

It was difficult for us to get on with our neighbours. We were twenty-one of us in the ward. On my left slept the artist; on the other side a big fellow, a bugler, whose face was as pitted as a thimble and as yellow as a glass of gall. He united two trades, that of a cobbler by day and procurer of loose women at night. He was very funny, however, and skipped about on his head or hands; with the utmost naïveté he told us how, while cobbling, he attended to his saucepans; with a touching voice he sang a sentimental song:

> The only friend that I have kept
> In my misfortunes is a swallow.

I obtained his good graces by giving him twenty sous to buy a book, and we were fortunate in being on good terms with him, as the other occupants of the room, several of whom were solicitors on the rue Maubuée, were much inclined to pick quarrels with us.

One evening, for instance, on August 15, Francis Emonot threatened to do violence to two men who had cribbed his towel. A formidable uproar ensued in the dormitory. Insults followed in quick succession, they calling us "cads!" or "duchesses!" As we were only two against nineteen, we were about to receive a sound thrashing, when the bugler interposed, took the most infuriated men aside and coaxed them into returning the stolen towel. To celebrate the reconciliation that followed this scene, Francis and I contributed three francs each, and it was agreed that the bugler, with the help of his comrades, would slip out and bring back meat and wine.

The light had disappeared from the chief surgeon's window, the dispenser had at last put out his lamp, when we crawled out beyond the thickets, looked around, and signalled to the men. They glided along the walls, met with no sentinel on the way, and mounting on each other's shoulders, jumped into the open. An hour later they came back with provisions galore, which were passed on to us, and we all returned to the dormitory. The two night-lights were extinguished, candle-ends were lighted on the floor and we formed a circle round my bed in our night-shirts. We had absorbed three or four litres of wine and cut up more than half of a leg of mutton, when a great noise of boots was heard. I put out the candle-ends with my slipper and we all hid under the beds.

The door flew open, the chief surgeon appeared and uttered a formidable oath, tripped in the dark, walked out and came back with a lantern accompanied by his inevitable train of attendants. I had taken advantage of the interval to clear away the remains of the feast. The surgeon crossed the dormitory at quick step, swearing and threatening to have us arrested and confined to barracks.

We were indulging in fits of laughter under our bedclothes when a flourish of trumpets resounded at the end of the room. The chief surgeon placed us all on a strict diet and left us with a warning that in a few moments we would know what kind of stuff he was made of.

As soon as he was gone we all roared: peals of laughter burst out, hilarious rockets were fired; the bugler turned over on his hands and feet, a friend of his imitating him; a third jumped on his bed like on a springboard, bounding, rebounding, waving his arms while his night-shirt flew about him. The man next to him was beginning to kick up a triumphant *cancan,* when all of a sudden the chief surgeon reappeared, ordered four linesmen he had brought with him to collar the dancers and announced that he would make a report, to be sent to the proper authorities.

At last quiet was restored. The next day we induced the assistants to buy us some victuals. Days passed without further incident. We were getting bored to death, when one morning at five o'clock the doctor rushed in and ordered us to don our accoutrements and buckle on our knapsacks.

Ten minutes later we heard that the Prussians were marching on Châlons. Dull stupor fell on the dormitory. Until then we had had no idea of what was going on. We had been apprised of the too celebrated victory at Sarrebrück and were far from expecting such overwhelming reverses. The chief surgeon examined each one of us: none were well, all had been too long saturated with liquo-rice-water and treated with scant attention. He nevertheless sent the most fit to their respective corps and ordered the remainder to lie down in their clothes with their knapsacks ready. Francis and I were among the latter. A day went by followed by a night without incident; but I was still suffering severely from my bowels. At last, about 9 a.m., a long line of mule ambulances led by Mobiles appeared. We both climbed into panniers. Francis and I had hoisted each other on the same mule; only as the artist was very stout and I very emaciated, the apparatus gave way: up I went into the air, while he went down under the belly of the beast, which, being pulled along in front and pushed from behind, kicked and plunged furiously. We ran along in a whirlpool of dust, blinded, flurried, tossed about, clinging to the bar of the ambulance, closing our eyes, laughing and moaning by turns. We reached Châlons more dead than alive and fell down on the sand like worn-out cattle. We were then huddled into railway carriages and rolled away from the town, nobody knew whither.

Night had closed: we flew along the rails. The sick left their seats and stood on the platforms.

We heard the engine whistle, the train slackened its speed and came to a stop at a station, Rheims station, I suppose, but I could not swear to it. We were dying of hunger: the commissariat had only forgotten one thing, which was to provide us with loaves for the journey. I alighted, and finding a refreshment-room open I ran in. Others had got there first: they were already fighting together on my arrival. Some seized bottles, others viands, bread, cigars. The owner, driven mad, defended his establishment furiously, armed with a jug. Pushed on by their comrades who came on in a crowd, the first line of Mobiles crashed into the counter, which gave way, dragging down in its fall the boss and his waiters. Then began a regular pillage. Nothing escaped; even matches and toothpicks were pinched. Meanwhile a bell rang and the train started. No one had taken any notice. While seated on the line I explained to the artist, whose bronchial tubes gave him trouble, the composition of the various parts of a sonnet; the train backed to pick us up.

We entrained once more and reckoned up the conquered booty. I must say the provisions lacked variety, they all came from a pork-butcher's shop, there was nothing but what such a shop offers: we had six saveloys seasoned with garlic, a scarlet tongue, two large sausages, a grand slice of Bologna sausage, a silver-lined slice of Lyons sausage, of dark red meat interlarded with white fat, four litres of wine, half a bottle of cognac and some candle-ends. The last we fixed in the necks of our water-bottles, which swung, tied by strings to the sides of the carriage. Now and then, when the train crossed the points of a siding with a jump, down came a shower of hot drops which hardened almost immediately, forming broad patches of grease on our clothes, but these had already suffered on many other occasions. We at once began the repast, which was interrupted by the coming and going of Mobiles, who, running all along the foot-boards of the train, knocked at our windows for something to drink. We sang at the top of our voices, drank and touched glasses; never did sick travellers indulge in such noise and such frolicking on board a train. You would have thought yourself in a rolling Court of Miracles where cripples jumped close-legged, where men whose bowels were burning cooled them with draughts of cognac, and those who had but one eye opened two, where the feverish cut capers and people with sore throats bawled and tippled. It was an unheard-of experience.

The turbulence subsided after a while. I took advantage of this moment of quiet to put my head out of the window. There was not a star to be seen, not the slightest glimpse of the moon; heaven and earth seemed one, and in the intense darkness the lanterns hanging from the sheet-iron signals winked like eyes of different colours. The engine whistled, the funnel smoked and vomited sparks continuously. I closed the window and looked at my companions. Some were snoring, the others, inconvenienced by the jolts, grumbled and swore, turning from side to side, trying to find room to stretch their legs and rest their heads, which every jolt disturbed.

Tired out by the long watching, I began to slumber, when I was roused by the train coming to a standstill. We were in a station, and the station-master's office flared like the fire of a forge in the darkness of the night. One of my legs was benumbed and I was shivering with cold. I got down to warm myself a little. I walked up and down the line and went to see the engine, which they were uncoupling to attach another, and passing by the telegraph office I listened to the ringing and ticking of the apparatus. The clerk had his back turned to me, and as he leaned a little to the right, I could only see, from where

I stood, the back of his head and the tip of his nose, which shone red and perspiring, while what remained of his face disappeared in the shadow cast by the shade of a gas-light. I was ordered back to the carriage, where I found my comrades as I had left them. This time I went off to sleep. How long I slumbered I could not tell. A loud shout awoke me: Paris! Paris! I rushed to the window. In the distance stood out in black on a pale gold streak the chimneys of factories and mills. It was St. Denis. The news spread from carriage to carriage. All stood while the train still hurried on. The Gare du Nord loomed from afar: on arriving there we ran to the exits: some managed to escape, others were stopped by the railway officials and the military. We were pushed into a train which was getting up steam, and God alone knew our destination now.

Again we rolled on for a whole day. I was sick of looking at those long files of houses and trees flying out of sight; moreover, my bowels still caused me pain. Towards four o'clock in the afternoon the train slowed and stopped at a platform where we were received by an old General around whom fluttered a flock of young men in pink képis, red trousers and boots with golden spurs. The general inspected us and divided us into two parties, of which one marched to the Seminary and the others were sent to the hospital. We were told that the town was Arras. Francis and I were in the former party. They hoisted us on carts filled with straw and we reached a large building which seemed to be sinking and about to fall into the street. We ascended to a room on the second floor containing about thirty beds. Each unbuckled his knapsack, combed his hair and sat down. A doctor entered.

"What's the matter with you?" he said to the first.

"A carbuncle."

"Ah! and you?"

"Dysentery."

"Ah! and you?"

"A bubo."

"I see: you have not been wounded in the war?"

"Not in the least."

"Well, then, you may put your knapsacks on again. The archbishop only gives the seminarists' beds to the wounded."

I put back into my knapsack the odds and ends I had taken out, and we trudged as well as we could to the town hospital. Here there was no more room. In vain did the Sisters try to get the iron bedsteads closer, the wards had their full complement. Impatient of these delays, I laid hold of a mattress, Francis took another and we went to lie down on a large lawn in the garden.

The next morning I had a talk with the director, an affable and charming man. I asked him to permit the artist and myself to go into the town, which request he granted. The door was opened and we were free! At last we could enjoy a good breakfast, eat real meat, drink genuine wine! What a treat! Without dallying we set out for the best hotel in the town. A succulent repast was served. There were flowers on the table, beautiful bouquets of roses and fuschias that bloomed in high glass vases! The waiter brought us a rib of beef exuding its juice into a lake of butter. The sun joined in the festivity, making the silver and knives shine, sifting its golden rays through the decanters and caressing the Pommard which at every movement swayed gently to and fro in the glasses, colouring with a ruddy spot the damask table-cloth.

O heavenly joy of a copious meal! My mouth was full for once and Francis was tipsy! The flavour of the roast meat mixed with the perfume of the flowers, the purple wine tried to outshine the blushing roses, the waiter looked like a real idiot and we like gormandizers; but little did we care, we crammed roast upon roast, and gulped draughts of claret, burgundy, chartreuse and cognac. Away with the bad wines and atrocious spirits we had ingurgitated since we had left Paris! The devil take those unnamable drinks, those unheard of dishes with which we had filled ourselves for nearly a month! We were now unrecognizable, our famished faces were all aglow, we brawled defiantly as we staggered through the town.

When evening came, we had perforce to go back to the hospital. The Sister in charge of the old people's ward said to us in her gentle, flute-like voice:

"Gentlemen, you were very cold last night, now you are going to have a warm bed."

She led us to a large ward where three night-lights threw their miserable rays on the ceiling. My bed had white sheets. It was a delight to plunge into linen fresh from the wash. Soon nothing was heard but breathing and snoring. I felt too hot; my eyes closed; I had lost all sense of my whereabouts, when a prolonged clucking sound roused me. I opened one eye and perceived at the foot of my bed an individual who was staring at me. I sat up and saw before me a tall and lean old man with hollow eyes, from whose lips dribble fell upon an unkempt beard. I inquired what he wanted, and receiving no reply I cried out: "Go away! let me sleep!"

He threatened me with his fist. Suspecting him to be out of his mind, I rolled up a towel, one end of which I furtively knotted. He advanced a step, I jumped out of bed, parried the blow aimed at me, answering it with a swing of the towel that struck his left eye. Although stunned, he made a dash for me: I retreated after landing him a vigorous kick in the stomach. Down he fell, pulling over a chair, which rebounded. The noise awoke the whole dormitory. Francis in his night-shirt hurried to my assistance, the Sister appeared, the attendants rushed at the madman, gave him a beating, and with much trouble got him into bed.

The dormitory offered a fantastic sight: the vague rosy glimmer shed around by the dying night-lights had been succeeded by the bright flashes of three lanterns; the dark ceiling, lighted only by round spots that danced above the burning wicks, now shone bright, as if it had just been whitewashed. The inmates, old fogies whose ages were a mystery, had laid hold of the wooden bars hanging by a rope above their beds and clung to them with one hand, while with the other they made fearful gestures. At this sight my anger relaxed, I burst out laughing, the artist nearly choked. The Sister alone kept a serious countenance and succeeded by threats and entreaties in re-establishing order. We got through the night as well as we could, and in the morning at six o'clock the rolling of a drum brought us together and the director of the hospital called the roll. We were off to Rouen.

On our arrival there, an officer told the poor fellow who showed us the way that the hospital was absolutely full; so we had to wait an hour at the station. I threw my knapsack into a corner, and in spite of the grumbling of my inside, Francis and I roamed about without any direct purpose in view. But into what an ecstasy we fell when we beheld the church of St. Ouen! How we enjoyed the romantic old houses! We were so lost in admiration that we only thought of returning to the station long after the hour of departure had struck. "Your comrades have left long ago," said a railway official, "they are at Evreux!"

"The deuce! The first train will only be in at nine o'clock. Meantime let us dine!"

When we arrived at Evreux the night had closed in. It was too late to ask for admission at the hospital, they would have taken us for evil-doers. The night being fine we walked across the town and soon found ourselves in the open country. It was hay-making time: the ground was covered with bundles of hay. On seeing a small haystack we made ourselves two comfortable niches, and I cannot tell whether owing to the overpowering smell of our beds or to the penetrating fragrance of the woods, we felt it a necessity to go over our past love affairs, an inexhaustible subject! Little by little, however, the conversation slackened, enthusiasm cooled down and we fell asleep. "Good heavens!" cried my pal, stretching his limbs, "what time can it be?" His exclamation woke me. The sun was on the point of rising, the great blue curtain was already fringed with red on the horizon. Oh, misery! we would ere long have to knock at the hospital door and sleep in wards impregnated by the morbid odour of iodoform powder, that smells like an acrid flower never to be got rid of.

We sadly wended our way there. At the door, alas! Francis alone was admitted and I was dispatched to the lycée. Life was no longer to be endured, and I was meditating my escape, when one day the house-physician on duty came into the yard. I showed him my card of admission to the Law School. He knew Paris and the Latin Quarter, I explained the situation. "It is absolutely necessary," said I, "that Francis should come to the lycée or that I should join him at the hospital." He thought it over, and coming to my bed in the evening, he whispered these words: "Tell them tomorrow morning that you are worse." The doctor appeared the next day at about seven o'clock. He was a kindly, excellent man with only two faults: his breath was not rosy and he always wanted to get rid of his patients at any cost. The following scene was witnessed every day:

"Ah! ah! the sly fellow," he cried, "how well he looks! good complexion, no fever; leave your bed and get a good cup of coffee; but no nonsense, if you please, no running after petticoats; I am going to sign your discharge papers; tomorrow you will join your regiment." He used to send away three every day whether they were ill or not. On that morning he stopped at me and said:

"Good gracious, how much better you look, my boy!"

"I have never suffered so much," I exclaimed. —After tapping all over my stomach, he muttered: "But you are better; it is less hard." I protested. As he appeared astonished, the house-doctor whispered to him: "We ought perhaps to clear his bowels, but we have no instruments here; suppose we sent him to the hospital?"

"Ah! that's an idea," said the good man, enchanted to get rid of me, and there and then he signed my card of transfer. Beaming with joy, I buckled my knapsack, and I was taken to the hospital by a lycée assistant. Again with Francis! By rare good luck there was a vacant bed next to his in the corridor of St. Vincent where he slept, the wards being quite full. We were at last together! Besides our two beds five palliasses were aligned along the ochre-washed walls. They were occupied by a linesman, two artillery-men, a dragoon and a hussar. The rest of the inmates comprised a few cranky and whining old men, a few young ones, affected with rickets or crooked-legged, and a large number of soldiers who, like wreckage from MacMahon's army, after having rolled from one dressing station to another, had been left stranded in this place. Only Francis and I wore the uniform of Mobiles of the Seine. Our neighbours were not bad sorts, but each proved more insignificant than the other. They were mostly sons of peasants or farmers who had rejoined their regiments when war was declared.

While I was doffing my tunic, a Sister came towards me, looking so delicate, so pretty, that I could not keep my eyes off her. She had beautiful large eyes fringed with long fair lashes and what pretty teeth! She asked me why I had left the lycée. I explained as diplomatically as I could that they had sent me away because they had no forcing pump. She smiled gently and said: "Oh! sir, you might have called the instrument by its name, we are used to everything."

She must indeed have been used to everything, yet I never saw her blush; she passed among them without saying a word, looking down, pretending not to hear the vulgar jokes made by those around her.

How she spoilt me! I can still see her in the morning, while the sun dispelled the shadow of the window bars on the flagstones, advancing slowly towards me from the end of the corridor, the flappers of her coif flying about her face. She came to my bed with a steaming soup-plate, on the edge of which shone her well-shaped nail. "As the soup is rather thin this morning," she would say with her pretty smile, "I have brought you some chocolate instead; take it quickly while it is warm."

In spite of all her kindness I was bored to death. My friend and I sank to such a low state of spirits that we remained in bed to drowse away, like beasts, the long, unbearable hours. Our sole distractions were a lunch and dinner consisting of boiled beef, watermelon, prunes and a drop of wine, all in insufficient quantity to satisfy a man's appetite.

Owing to my simple politeness towards the Sisters and to my writing pharmaceutical labels for them, I had the good fortune to obtain a cutlet from time to time, and a pear from the hospital orchard. I was, therefore, on the whole, the least to be pitied of all the soldiers who crowded the wards. Yet I could not, during the first days, swallow my morning pittance, for it was visiting time and the doctor had chosen that moment for his operations. The second day after my arrival he slit open a thigh from top to bottom. I heard a heart-rending cry and closed my eyes; but I had seen a rain of red drops splash over his apron; no eating after that! Little by little, however, I became used to such scenes; I just turned my head away and protected my soup from accident. Meanwhile the situation became intolerable. Having tried in vain to obtain newspapers and books, we amused ourselves by putting on the hussar's jacket for fun; but this childish gaiety only lasted for a little, and we lay down again every twenty minutes, and after exchanging a few words buried our heads in our pillows. Conversation was impossible with our comrades. The two artillery-men and the hussar were too ill to talk; the dragoon swore without speaking, got up at every moment, wrapped in his large white cloak, and went to the lavatory, from which he brought back the smell of the malodorous liquid in which his bare feet had stood. The hospital lacked certain night vessels: some of the worst patients had, however, under their beds an old saucepan which the convalescents tossed like cooks, offering the contents to the Sisters as a joke.

There only remained the linesman, an unfortunate grocer's assistant who was father of a boy. He had been recalled to his regiment, was a constant prey to fever, and shivered under his bed-clothes.

Squatting tailor fashion on our beds, we listened to his account of the battle he had taken part in.

He had happened to be near Froeschwiller, on a plain surrounded by woods, and had seen red flashes through bursts of white smoke; he had kept his head down, trembling, terrified by the cannonade and the whistling bullets. He had trudged among the regiments over clayey ground without espying a single Prussian, not knowing where he was, hearing, close to him, groans interrupted by short cries. The ranks in front of him had suddenly turned back and in the bustle of the flight he had been thrown down, he knew not how. He had got up and taken to his heels, abandoning his gun and knapsack. At last, exhausted by a week's forced marches, worn out by terror and weakened by hunger, he had sat down in a ditch. There he had remained stupefied, without movement, deafened by the crashing of the shells, determined not to defend himself any longer nor budge an inch. Then he had thought of his wife; and asking himself with tears why he had been made to suffer this agony, he had unconsciously picked up a leaf which he had kept, which he prized, for he often pulled it out of some pocket, dried and shrivelled, to show us. An officer had come by, revolver in hand, calling him a coward and threatening to blow out his brains if he did not march on. "I prefer that," he had replied, "let that be the end!" But the officer, while shaking him to get him on his legs, had toppled over and blood had trickled down his nape. Then, seized again by fear, he had taken to flight and, succeeded in reaching a distant road crowded with fugitives, black with troops, furrowed by teams whose terrified horses broke the ranks in their fall.

At last they had found shelter. From groups arose the cry of treason. Veteran soldiers still made a show of resolution, but the recruits refused to continue the fight. "Let them go and be killed," they said, "that's their job!—I have children, the State won't feed them when I am dead." And they envied the fate of those who were slightly wounded and who could find refuge in the dressing stations. "How frightened one is! How long one keeps hearing the voices of those who call for their mothers and beg for a drink!" he added, shuddering. He remained silent a while, and looking at the corridor with rapture, he continued: "All the same, I am glad to be here, for now my wife can write to me," and from his pocket he pulled out letters, saying with pleasure: "The little fellow has written, look," and he showed us at the foot of a page, under the laborious scrawl of his wife, strokes forming a dictated sentence which contained several times, amid blots of ink, the words "I kiss daddy."

We heard this yarn at least twenty times and for mortal hours we had to endure the tiresome twaddle of this poor fellow who was so delighted to have a son. At length we stopped our ears and tried to go to sleep so as not to hear him any longer.

This deplorable situation threatened to go on indefinitely, when one morning Francis, who contrary to his habit had roamed about the yard the whole day before, said to me: "Hullo, Eugène, will you come and have a breath of country air?" I pricked up my ears. "There is a yard," he went on, "reserved for the mad; it is not in use at present;

by climbing on the roof of the padded cells, which is easy to do, thanks to the window gratings, we can reach the top of the wall: a jump, and we are in the country. The wall is close to one of the gates of Evreux. What do you say?"

"I say . . . I say that I am quite ready for an outing, but how shall we get back?"

"That I don't know: let us be off and think it over later on. Get up, they will soon bring the soup; immediately after we shall scale the wall."

I left my bed. As water was scarce at the hospital, I had to wash myself with Seltzer which the Sister had obtained for me. I aimed with the siphon at the artist, who cried: "Fire!" The lever was depressed and the water squirted into his face. Then I stood and received in turn a spurt upon my beard. I rubbed my nose with the froth and wiped myself dry. As soon as ready we went down to the deserted yard and climbed the wall. Francis took sufficient start and jumped. I was astride the top. I looked around: below was a grassy ditch, to the right one of the gates of the town; in the distance the frizzly outline of a forest stood out against a pale blue streak. I stood up, and hearing some noise in the yard, I jumped. Then gliding along the wall, we entered Evreux.

"Suppose we have something to eat?"

"Right you are."

On the way in search of a lodging, we perceived two young women skimming along: we followed them and offered them a *déjeuner.* They refused, we insisted; then they declined our invitation less decidedly. We insisted again and they accepted. We brought a meat pie, various bottles, eggs and a cold chicken to their lodgings. How extraordinary it appeared to us to be in a bright room having a wallpaper of lilac flowers and green leaves, and window curtains of light green damask! The mantelpiece was adorned with a mirror, an engraving representing Christ pestered by Pharisees; there were six chairs of wild cherry wood; a round table covered with oil-cloth on which were painted the kings of France; over the bed was spread an eiderdown of pink cambric muslin. We put up the table and looked greedily at the girls bustling around it. It took a long time to lay the table, as we kissed them each time they passed. They were ugly and stupid, but what did that matter? We had not tasted women's lips for such a time!

I cut up the chicken and bottles were uncorked; we drank like choristers and guzzled like ogres. Coffee steamed in the cups and was gilded with cognac. Away flew my sadness! The punch was set fire to: the blue flames of the kirsch fluttered in the crackling salad-bowl; the girls became merry; their dishevelled hair flew about their eyes; their charms became irresistible. Suddenly four strokes resounded slowly from the church bell; it was four o'clock. Good heavens! we had forgotten the hospital. I turned pale; Francis looked at me with dismay; we tore ourselves from our hostesses' arms and hurried out.

"How shall we get in?" said the artist.

"Alas! we have no choice, we shall barely arrive in time for the soup. Let's chance it and slip in by the front door!"

We rang the bell: the Sister who attended the door opened it and stood aghast. We saluted her and I said, loud enough for her to hear:

"I say, do you know that the commissariat officials are not too amiable? The stout one in particular received us with scant politeness."

The Sister made no remark. We galloped up to the dormitory; it was high time, I could hear the voice of Sister Angèle distributing the rations. I hastened to my bed, taking care to cover with my hand a bruise which the damsel had left on my neck. The Sister looked at me, found my eyes inordinately excited and said with concern:

"Do you feel worse?"

I reassured her, replying: "On the contrary, I feel better, Sister, but this idleness and imprisonment are killing me."

Whenever I complained to her of the dreadful lassitude I experienced feeling alone among such company, in the remotest corner of a province, far from my own people, she made no reply, but tightened her lips, her eyes expressing indefinable melancholy and pity. And yet one day she had said to me dryly: "No! liberty would not be a good thing for you," alluding to a conversation she had overheard between Francis and me, in which we discussed the gay charms of Parisian ladies. Then in a gentler tone she had added, pouting in her charming little way:

"You are really not serious enough, my dear soldier."

Next morning the painter and I agreed that after swallowing our soup we would again scale the wall. At the hour decided upon we prowled around the yard: the door was shut. "So much the worse!" exclaimed Francis, "on we go!" and he made for the chief entrance. I followed him. The nun in charge of the door asked where we were going.—"To the commissariat." She opened the door and we were free.

On reaching the market-place in front of the church, I noticed, while we examined the sculptures of the porch, a stout gentleman whose round, red face bristled with a white moustache; he looked at us with astonishment. We stared at him unblushingly and went our way. As Francis was dying with thirst, we entered a café, and while sipping a half-glass, I perused a local paper and came across a name that set me musing. I was not, to say the truth, acquainted with the person that bore it, but this name reawoke remembrances that had slumbered a long time. A friend of mine had a relative of high station who lived at Evreux. "I must pay her a visit," I said to the artist. I asked the café keeper for his address: he did not know it. I inquired at all the bakers' and chemists' shops I passed. As everybody eats bread and takes potions, thought I, it is impossible that one of these should not know the address of M. de Fréchède. This surmise proved correct. After brushing my tunic, I bought a black tie and some gloves and made for the Rue Chartraine. I rang gently at the gate of a mansion which reared its brick façades and its slate roofs in the midst of a sunny park. A valet showed me in. M. de Fréchède was absent, but Madame was at home. I had been waiting for a few moments in a drawing-room, when a door-curtain was lifted and an elderly lady appeared. Reassured by her very affable look, I explained in a few words who I was.

"Sir," she said with a kindly smile, "I have heard a good deal about your family; I even believe I have seen your mother at Madame Lezant's the last time I went to Paris. You are welcome."

We had a long talk, I, not quite at ease, hiding with my képi the mark on my neck, she trying to make me accept money, which I refused.

"Come," she said at last, "I wish with all my heart to be useful to you. What can I do?"

"Ah! madame," I replied, "if you could obtain from the authorities permission for my return to Paris, you would render me a great service. According to the papers, communications are soon to be cut, and they foresee a new coup d'état or the fall of the Empire. I wish very much to join my mother and above all not to remain here as a prisoner in case the Prussians come."

Thereupon M. de Fréchède entered the room. In a few words he was informed of the situation.

"If you wish to come with me to the hospital doctor," he said, "we have no time to lose."

To the doctor! Good heavens! Could I explain to him how I had left the place? I dared not utter a word and followed my protector, asking myself how it would all end. The doctor looked at me with astonishment. Leaving him no time to open his mouth, I treated him, with marvellous volubility, to a long jeremiad, concerning my sad predicament.

M. de Fréchède spoke in his turn and asked him to grant me a two months' convalescent leave.

"The gentleman is evidently quite ill enough," said the doctor, "to claim two months of rest; if my colleagues and the General accept my view, your protégé will be allowed to return to Paris in a few days."

"Excellent!" replied M. de Fréchède, "I thank you, doctor; this evening I shall speak to the General."

Once in the street, I heaved a heavy sigh of relief, I grasped the hand of the excellent man who had deigned to take an interest in me, and I ran to seek Francis. We had just time enough to get back. Francis rang at the hospital gate; I saluted the Sister. "Did you not tell me this morning," she interrupted, "that you were going to the commissariat?"

"Certainly, my Sister."

"Well, the General has just left. Go to the director and Sister Angèle, who are waiting for you;

you will no doubt explain to them the object of your visits to the commissariat."

Quite out of countenance, we walked up the dormitory stairs. Sister Angèle, who was waiting for me, exclaimed:

"I would never have believed it! You have been running about the whole town yesterday and to-day, and God knows what sort of life you have led!"

"How can you say such things!" I rejoined.

She looked at me so fixedly that I was struck dumb.

"It's true all the same," she continued; "the General met you today on the market-place. I declared you had not been out and searched for you all over the hospital. The General was right: you were out. He asked for your names: I only gave him one and refused to tell the other. This was a mistake on my part, for you do not deserve it."

"Oh! Sister, how grateful I am!" . . . But Sister Angèle was not listening, she was indignant at my conduct! There was nothing else for me to do but to remain silent and to bear the storm without seeking shelter. Meanwhile Francis was summoned to the director's room, and as, for some reason or other, they suspected him of corrupting me, and in consequence of his unseemly jokes he was not in the good graces of either doctor or Sisters, he was told to join his corps the next day.

"The hussies with whom we lunched yesterday are simply authorized prostitutes who have sold us," Francis affirmed in a fury: "the doctor told me so himself."

While we cursed these wenches and deplored that our uniforms should have betrayed us so easily, the rumour spread that the Emperor had been made a prisoner and that the Republic had been proclaimed at Paris. I gave a franc to an old inmate who had leave to go out, asking him to get me a number of the *Gaulois*. The news was true: the hospital rejoiced. "Badinguet was done for and not too soon! At last the war is at an end!" we cried.

Next morning Francis and I embraced, and as he went off, he shouted: "Au revoir! Get you to Paris!" and shut the gate. Oh! what days succeeded, what sufferings and despair! I could not leave the hospital, as a sentry marched up and down before the entrance in my honour. I had, however, the courage not to give way to sleep and walked about the yard like a beast in a cage. I roamed thus for twelve hours. I had studied every corner of my prison, I knew where wall plants and mosses abounded, where the wall was cracked and creviced. I was disgusted with the corridor, with my bed that was as flat as a pancake, with the obstinate whiner, and with my linen rotting from dirt. I lived apart, not speaking to a soul, kicking about the stones in the yard, wandering like a tormented spirit under the arcades washed with ochre, the same as the walls of the wards, returning to the entrance gate surmounted by a flag, ascending to the first floor and my bed, going down to the kitchen where the utensils shone, the red copper saucepans darting rays in the dim light. Impatience made me champ the bit as I witnessed at certain hours civilians and soldiers going and coming, passing and repassing on every floor, crowding the galleries as they crawled along.

I had not even strength enough to elude the Sisters, who were bent on beating us up for chapel on Sundays. I was becoming a monomaniac, obsessed as I was by the idea of escaping as soon as possible from this lamentable gaol. My mother had sent me a hundred francs to Dunkerque, where she imagined me to be. This money was not forwarded, and I saw the moment when I would not have a sou to buy tobacco or paper. Day after day the de Fréchèdes seemed to have forgotten me, and I attributed their silence to my escapades, which no doubt they had heard of. These agonies of mind were accompanied by horrible physical pain. My bowels, unattended to and irritated during my escapades, were burning. I suffered to such a degree that I feared I should not be able to stand the fatigues of the journey. Yet I dissembled my sufferings for fear that the doctor might detain me by force. I kept to my bed several days; then, feeling that my strength was giving way, I determined to get up and went down into the yard.

Sister Angèle never spoke to me, and in the evening, as she made her round in the corridors and dormitories, looking aside so as not to notice the pipes gleaming in the dark, she passed before me, indifferent and cold, turning away her eyes.

On a certain morning, however, as I was dragging myself about the yard, letting myself sink on every bench, she noticed that I was so changed and pale, and she could not restrain a feeling of compassion.

In the evening, after she had been round the dormitories, I was leaning on my bolster, gazing at the bluish beams which the moon shed through the corridor-windows, when the door at the further end of the ward opened again and I perceived Sister Angèle coming towards me, and as she passed before the windows or the walls she appeared bathed in a silvery mist, or as a dark figure in black crape. "Tomorrow morning," she said with a gentle smile, "you are to be examined by the doctors. I have seen Madame de Fréchède today and you will probably start for Paris in two or three days." I jumped up in my bed, my face brightened. I could have leaped about and sung, never had I been so happy. Next morning after dressing, not without some anxiety, I betook myself to the room where a number of officers and doctors were in council. One by one soldiers exhibited their hairy, bullet-scarred torsos. The General was filing one of his nails; the Colonel of gendarmes was fanning himself with a sheet of paper, the practitioners chatted while their fingers pressed the patients' bodies. My turn came at last: I was examined from head to foot; they felt my stomach which was swollen and inflated like a balloon, and the council unanimously granted me sixty days' convalescent leave. At last I was to see my mother again and find myself among my knick-knacks and books! A red-hot iron no longer burned my bowels, and I skipped about like a kid!

I advised my family of the good news. My mother wrote letter on letter wondering why I did not come. Alas! my papers had to be endorsed at the Rouen division. I received them five days later and now all was in order. I went to beg Sister Angèle to obtain for me, before the time fixed for my departure, a permit to go and thank the de Fréchèdes who had been so kind to me. She brought me the permit granted by the director. I hurried to the house of those good people. They obliged me to accept a silk handkerchief and fifty francs for my travelling expenses. At the commissariat I was provided with a travelling permit. At the hospital I had but a few minutes to dispose of, and tried to find Sister Angèle; she was in the garden. I said to her with much emotion: "Dear Sister, I am off! How shall I ever be able to show you my gratitude?" I seized her hand, which she wanted to draw back, and lifted it to my lips: she blushed. "Adieu," she murmured, and with a threatening finger she added gaily: "Be a good boy, and especially avoid bad company on the journey."

"Oh! fear nothing of the sort, Sister, I promise to do my best!" At the appointed hour the entrance gate was opened, I rushed to the station and jumped into a carriage: the train started and I had left Evreux. The compartment was only half full and I took possession of a corner seat. Looking out of the window I saw a few pollarded trees and low hills winding in the distance; a bridge crossed a large pool that sparkled in the sun like a pane of glass; it was no joyous scene. I sunk back in my corner, casting now and again a look at the telegraph wires that ruled the background with dark lines. The train stopped. The travellers who were around me alighted, the door was closed and then reopened and a young woman entered the compartment.

While she sat down and uncrumpled her dress, I caught a glimpse of her face, thanks to the fluttering of her veil. She was charming, her eyes full of a heavenly blue, her lips tinged with carmine, her teeth white, her hair the colour of ripe maize. I started on a conversation: her name was Reine and she embroidered flowers; we chatted like old friends. She suddenly became pale and seemed about to swoon. I opened the ventilators and handed her a smelling bottle I had brought from Paris in case of need; she thanked me, saying it was nothing and leaned on my knapsack to try to sleep. Happily we were alone; but the wooden barrier that divided the carriage into two compartments was only waist high and one could hear the shouts and loud laughter of country men and women. I could have beaten these fools who disturbed her sleep. I had to be content with listening to the silly political views they exchanged, and

I soon had enough. I stopped my ears and tried to go to sleep; but the words uttered by the station-master at the last stoppage, "You will not get as far Paris, the line has been cut at Mantes," constantly disturbed my slumber, like the repeated burden of a song. I opened my eyes; my companion awoke; I kept my fears to myself. We talked in whispers: she told me she would meet her brother at Sèvres. "But," said I, "the train will not enter Paris before 11 p.m. You will never have time to reach the departure platform on the left bank of the Seine."

"What shall I do," she replied, "if my brother is not there to meet me?"

Oh, misery! I was as grimy as could be, my stomach was all afire! I could not think of taking her to a bachelor's lodgings, and besides I wished first to run to my mother's. How to manage? I looked anxiously at Reine and took her hand. At this moment the train changed to another line; the jolt threw her forward, bringing our lips together; I quickly impressed mine on hers and she turned crimson. Good heavens! her mouth moved imperceptibly and she returned my kiss; a long thrill ran along my back; at the contact of these glowing lips I felt ready to faint. Ah! Sister Angèle, Sister Angèle, a man cannot change his nature!

The train roared and rolled on at full speed, we were flying towards Mantes. Contrary to my apprehension the line was free. Reine half closed her eyes, her head dropped on my shoulder; her little curls mixed with my beard and tickled my lips; I supported her supple waist and rocked her to and fro. We were nearing Paris: we passed docks and warehouses, circular work-shops where, in a glowing mist, engines roared, getting up steam. The train stopped, tickets were collected. After mature reflection I made up my mind first to take Reine to my bachelor lodgings, hoping that her brother would not be awaiting her arrival! We alighted: her brother was there.

"We shall meet in five days," she said, sending me a kiss, and the pretty bird flew off.

Five days after I was in bed terribly ill and the Prussians occupied Sèvres. I never saw her again. I heaved a heavy sigh, although it was no time for being sad.

Driven in a jolting cab, I recognized my quarter, arrived at my mother's house. I galloped up the stairs and rang hurriedly. The maid opened the door. "What! Monsieur!" she exclaimed, and ran to tell my mother, who rushed to meet me, turned pale, embraced me, examined me from head to foot, stepped back, looked at me and again hugged me.

Meanwhile the maid had emptied the sideboard. "You must be hungry, Monsieur Eugène," she said.

"I am indeed!" I replied.

I devoured everything they gave me and gulped large glasses of wine; to speak the truth, I did not know what I ate or drank. I returned to my lodgings for the night. I found my apartments just as I had left them, and went over them beaming with joy; then I sat down on the settee, where I remained in ecstasies, in raptures, gorging my eyes with the sight of my knick-knacks and books. After that I undressed and enjoyed a thorough washing, realizing that for the first time in months I would have a clean bed and clean feet and nails. I jumped into my billowing couch and buried my head in the feathery pillow; I closed my eyes and was soon sailing at full speed o'er the sea of dreams.

Methought I saw Francis lighting his large wooden pipe, Sister Angèle looking at me with her gentle pout, and Reine coming towards me. At this I started up, called myself a fool and sunk again into the pillow. But my abdominal pains which had ceased for a while made themselves felt as soon as my nerves grew quiet. I rubbed my stomach gently, happy at being released from the horrible predicament of those suffering from dysentery. I was at home, I could be sure of privacy, and I reflected that one must have lived in the promiscuity of hospitals and camps to appreciate the value of a basin of water, and to delight in the comfort of being able to look after oneself without being the target of every eye.

A PARTIAL LIST OF SNUGGLY BOOKS